the Beggars' christmas

the BEGGARS' christmas

John Aurelio

Illustrated by Stan Skardinski

Paulist Press • New York • Ramsey

Library of Congress
Catalog Card Number: 79-65893

ISBN: 0-8091-2221-9

Designed by Emil Antonucci

Published by Paulist Press
Editorial office: 1865 Broadway, New York, N.Y. 10023
Business office: 545 Island Road, Ramsey, N.J. 07446

Printed and bound in the
United States of America

1

It happened a long time ago — a long, long
time ago in the year twelve hundred and
thirty. The bishop ascended the pulpit of the
monastery church of Soissons. It was the
first Sunday of Advent — the season of
preparation. The Church was awaiting the
coming of Jesus.

"My people," he said in a solemn tone,
"we gather together to await the coming of
our Lord Jesus. May he come to us soon in
glory. May we long for his arrival as the world
once waited for his arrival at Bethlehem. Oh
how the world waited for its Savior. How it
longed for him to come and set it free. Free
from slavery. Free from pain and sickness.

1

Free to rejoice and celebrate. Free to love without fear or worry. This would take a great man. This would take a God-man. A mighty king. A great warrior who would battle against great powers and mighty thrones. A king of kings they awaited. He would come. They knew he would come. It was promised. And he came. Yes, my people, he came — but not as a king of kings. No, he came as the lowly son of a carpenter. He was born not in a regal castle but in a stable. His army was made up of shepherds. His court was composed of oxen and sheep. His ministers were the magi."

An air of awe filled the church. These were his people, his court. They were farmers and shepherds, weavers of wool, bakers of bread. They were his army and they listened. Their ears and their hearts listened.

"I have something wonderful to tell you. I have held it in my heart till I thought it would burst. Now the time is right and I will share the good news with you. As you know, this past year I made my appointed visit to His Holiness the Pope — may the Lord bless his reign. On my journey homeward I chanced to pass through the town of Assisi in Italy. There I met a holy man, Francis by name. The wonder of God was about this man, I tell you, and I spent many an hour in holy conversation with him. He did tell me of the most marvelous happening. While deep in meditation about the birth of our blessed Savior he was inspired by the Holy Spirit to make a depiction of the holy birth so that the

2

people would remember. Thereupon he called his people together and informed them of his revelation. This last Christmas, people were chosen and, having dressed themselves appropriate to the time, they presented in tableau a living nativity. One was Joseph, another the Blessed Virgin. Still others were shepherds and the magi presenting their gifts of gold, frankincense, and myhrr. A new-born babe was placed in the manger to represent the Christ Child. Such a holy scene he pictured that the faithful felt as though they were in Bethlehem themselves. I tell you that as he spoke my heart was filled with joy and wonder that he could depict that holy scene and make it present today. I knew that I must bring this good news home to you, my friends, and that we too must do this wonder for our people. It is the season of Advent, the time of preparation. Let us do what that holy monk of Assisi has done. Let us here make a depiction of that holy night so that our people too might see the wonder of our God. We must seek among us those who would portray good Joseph and holy Mary. We must find shepherds and magi and a new-born babe. This we will do for the eve of Christmas, as they did, to give glory to God and give our people the wonder of Bethlehem."

The entire village was astir with excitement. Preparations were begun for the great day. The right transept of the monastery church was arranged to depict a stable, with a wooden stall and hay and a manger. A very pious young maiden was chosen to be Mary, and a goodly peasant would be her husband. It was decided further who would represent the shepherds and also the three kings. Even what animals would be brought had been decided upon. All was in readiness except for the babe who would be the Christ Child. Alas, in the entire village there was no new-born child. The nativity scene could not be finished without this most important person of all. The bishop, however, was not worried. "God will provide," he said. "Continue your preparations."

So at last the great day came—the eve of Christmas. All the villagers and people from the surrounding countryside gathered in the great church. Some people had come from as far away as Paris, having learned of what was scheduled.

In front of the church there was a holy scene indeed. It was as if Bethlehem had come to Soissons. Those entering the church gazed upon the scene in long and silent reverence. The bishop vested for the celebration of midnight Mass and took his place at the throne. He gazed at the nativity scene, his heart filled with joy. Like the holy man Francis, he had made Bethlehem come alive to his people. It was all there before them—all except the Christ Child. There was yet no babe. The hour approached midnight. Holy Mass was about to begin. There could be no Gloria, no bells, no singing without the child. God would provide.

II

In the beggars' camp outside the village, a number of shabbily dressed mendicants huddled close to an equally impoverished campfire. A crippled man, who was not as old as his looks made him appear, lay on his side with a twisted, unused leg stretched out before him. He poked at the dying fire with his crutch, mumbling under his breath. "Even, nature is stingy to beggars," he complained. The others paid no heed. Even talk was scarce in that gathering.

A blind man stumbled out of the darkness into the small circle of light, more sensing than hearing where he was, and joined the others at the fire. The village clock struck the hour of eleven. "It approaches the hour," one of them said. "The people will be on their way to midnight Mass." "This should be a good night for begging" another interjected. "The villagers will be filled with good will for Christmas. I hear tell that some people have come from as far away as Paris to see this thing that the bishop has done. We should go to see this for ourselves. I have a strange feeling that this is going to be a blessed night. Let us hurry to the church to see what profit the night holds for us."

"Run off like enchanted children," the lame man shouted. "You fools! You idiots! I will tell you what wonders the night holds for you. Pious peasants mumbling their Our Fathers will walk past you with eyes closed so as not to be repulsed by the sight of you. Those hypocrites! They would walk past an army of beggars and go within to give homage to the king of all beggars. The church is a gathering place of fools and you are the greater fools if you join them."

The blind man replied: "Curb your tongue, villain, or God will wither it like your leg! Have you not been punished enough, or are you like the stupid moth who flirts with the flame until he is consumed by it?" The others would have blocked their ears against the lame man's blasphemy, but they were too busy making haste to the village. Only the blind man remained behind to hear his invective.

"Hasten off, jackasses," he shouted after them. "Your alms will be the dung of peasants."

"Why do you speak so?" the blind man asked into the night. The lame man made ready to attack him but, seeing that the man's state was more pitiable than his own, he poked his anger at the fire instead.

"Why such bitterness," he continued, "and on this holy night?"

"Because I can't abide with fools, much less pious fools, on this or any other night."

"But this is the eve of Christmas."

"What is Christmas to me, blind man, or to you? It is just a day like any other day, no better. If anything, it's worse."

"Nay, friend, how could it be worse? It is a day for rejoicing. A day of peace and cheer."

"For those of good will," the lame man shot back.

"And have you no good will?"

"Good will for what? For this leg of mine that is twisted and gnarled like this crutch? Should I be of good cheer for a life that was young and strong and now is bent and broken? I have no blessings. Therefore I give none. I give back a curse for a curse."

"What of God? Have you no fear of God?"

"Fear of God, you say. If there is a God, then I say: Let him come down from his throne and save me. Let him save me from this misery. Let him save you too, my blind friend, for you are no better than I."

"It is true what you say. I am no better than you, but perhaps older and perhaps wiser. For I too have cursed and rebelled. Nor is sin a stranger to me, for we have walked side by side through these many years. I am a sinner. But I fear God and his judgment."

"Let his judgment come, old man, for I fear neither him nor his judgment. Nor do I fear the evil one, for my club would make short work of him too," he said lifting his crutch. "I fear only the cold which makes my pain unbearable; and this wretched fire gives me no warmth or relief." He poked the end of his stick into the dying fire. When it would yield no further flame, in anger and frustration he raised his crutch and in full swing brought it down heavily on the glowing coals. Again and again he beat the fire as though it were a wanton child, but it responded only with cries of spitting sparks and gasps of dry smoke.

When his fury was spent, he sat there breathing heavily. The sparks faded and the smoke blew away into the cold night air. As the smoke cleared, by the ever so dim light of the glowing embers the lame man saw a figure standing across the fire from him. This sudden appearance startled him so that he cried out in surprise. The blind man who sat there quietly throughout the ordeal responded to the startled cry. "What is it? What is wrong?"

Growing in courage, the crippled man challenged the spectre. "Who are you? Where did you come from? How did you get here?" The sound of his own voice gave him strength again. "Who are you, I say? Are you some demon the evil one has sent to take up my challenge? Then draw closer and I will cudgel you as I would him." He raised himself with his

crutch, shifted all his weight onto his good leg, and waved his stick menacingly.

The figure stepped slowly forward across the embers. "You have no fear of me," cried the beggar. "Nor have I any fear of you." With that he lifted his stick above his head and began to strike it down on the ghostly figure. From nowhere the spectre drew a sword and swung it up against the stick, severing it in two. The force of his effort brought the crippled man to his knees before the ghost. The blind man, frightened by the event, stood up and reached both arms out into the night. "What is it? What is happening? Who is there?" he cried.

The spectre spoke: "I am a messenger of God. I am his angel."

The blind man quickly withdrew his outstretched hands as if stung by some unseen fire. "Is it time?" he gasped. "Have you come for judgment?"

"It is time," the angel said, "and I have come for judgment."

The blind man fell back with fear, but the crippled beggar found his voice. "So it is over. So this is how it is to be. Then speak God's judgment and be done with it. This world has given me naught but pain and grief. I expect the next to be no different."

"Wait!" cried the blind man. "Why have you come on this night? Why this of all nights, this holy night? I have felt your presence many times. Yet you did not take me. Why then on this Christmas night? I sense a meaning to this, though I do not fathom it."

"The Holy One has seen your travail. He has compassion on you. It has been given to you to find Christmas — before the sentence. You have but to ask."

Having heard this pronouncement, the crippled man rose to the occasion. He was knowledgeable in the ways of crafty bargaining, for he had done much of it in his day. Perhaps he could outwit even this angel. "I take it, then, that since we are to find the meaning of Christmas, we might look anywhere for it."

"It is decreed," the angel replied.

"And for any length of time."

"So be it."

"But what of our judgment?" cried the blind man.

"It is yours to decide," said the angel.

"Then I decide to look for it in my youth," interrupted the other. "Then I shall have time enough to find it. As you said, any place and for any length of time."

"So be it," said the angel. He stretched out both his hands and with a touch like none of any mortal man, neither warm nor cold but like the kiss of a gentle breeze, he placed his hands on the shoulders of the two peasants. In an instant they were gone.

III

The three of them were standing on the
street of a small village that looked like so
many other villages of their day. They stood
before the open door of what certainly was a
bakery, for the sweet smell of bread filled the
air. The air itself was cold and crisp as
snowflakes gently blanketed the earth. The
blind man sensed but could not see the
change that had taken place.

"Where are we?" he asked.

"It is my village," cried out the lame man.
"And this is the bakery shop of my father. It
is now just as it was then. Can it be? Can
this be true?" He ran out into the street
feasting his eyes on the joy of the place. "It

15

is true," he shouted out, jumping up and down with merriment, his legs sound and whole.

"What is it, angel?" the blind man asked. "What has happened? Are you still here?"

"I am here," he replied.

"What is happening?"

"It is as he wished."

"But I cannot see."

"Let your ears see for you."

He heard the voice of a sweet gentle woman coming from the doorway of the bakery. "Look at your son," she laughed. "He's dancing in the street. I tell you, he has no head about him these days."

"It's love," came the masculine reply. "Our son has been struck with the madness of love."

"Love indeed!" she pretended to chide her husband for his permissiveness, for in truth this son of hers was the apple of her eye. "Who might be the object of this sudden madness?"

"You know full well it is the miller's daughter."

"The miller's daughter. She is only a child."

"Not so, good woman. She is nigh onto thirteen years and already sealed by the Church."

"And he is only a lad of fifteen — still too young for holy wedlock."

"Too young, yes, but soon, good woman, soon."

"Enough of this foolish talk." She would not

let herself think of it. "There is work to be done." She quietly busied herself kneading dough. The miller's daughter was a pretty girl at that. Her father too was a goodly man and would make a fine in-law. What better match for a baker's son than a miller's daughter? And to think she would be a grandmother. They would have many children who would come running to her for comfort and for her favors. The vision of her future set her to humming contentedly, until her reverie was interrupted by her husband. "Call in that favorite of yours," he said, careful that the other children were not about to hear it. She wiped her hands on her apron and walked to the doorway, glancing lovingly at her handsome young son gamboling merrily in the street.

"Will you play all day, my young stag?" she called out. "The bread is near done and your father asks for you."

"I am here," the boy announced as he bounded into the shop.

"Come within," his father said walking toward a back room. "I have matters to speak to you of in private, man to man." He winked at his wife.

The blind man and the angel were still standing at the doorway. "May we enter?" he asked. "We may," the angel answered, "for they can neither hear us nor see us." They followed the two into the back room where the baker began searching under the bed. Having found what he was looking for, he stood up and displayed it for his son to see.

17

It was a shawl—a fine, colorful, woven shawl.

"What do you think of it, my son?"

"It's beautiful, father."

"It's for your mother for Christmas. Do you think she will be pleased?"

"She will be filled with joy. It is the most beautiful shawl I have ever seen. She will be the talk of the village and the envy of all the women."

"I have other gifts too," he said, his face beaming—"gifts for everyone." Then he reached under the bed and brought out other surprises.

"This is for your sister and these are for your brothers," he said, naming each one, and proud and pleased over his eldest's praise of him. But he displayed no gift for him.

Then he looked into his son's questioning face and said: "Oh, I did not forget you, my son. For you it must be a man's gift. You are no longer a child."

"What is it, father?" he asked with the impetuosity of a child.

"After Christmas day," he paused tauntingly. "After Christmas day," he repeated, savoring the mounting excitement. Then he quickly blurted out: "You will accompany me to Paris." He let his words sink in. The boy stood disbelieving. Could it be? Would he really go to that great and wonderful city? All his young life he had never been beyond the village. Now the thought of going to Paris left him dumbstruck. Since the first day he had ever

19

heard of it, the city filled all his dreams. He had visions of the king's great palace and the golden gates that opened to it. He imagined armies of handsome uniformed soldiers with magnificent plumed hats riding their stately horses through the streets, and the shops of endless number and variety having for sale wondrous goods from all over the world. It was his one constant dream, his one ever present desire. Now it was to come true, and he stood there speechless.

"The woman was right," the baker said. "The boy is mad. Here I tell him the most wonderful news and he stands before me like a scarecrow."

The lad came to his senses with a screech of joy. He ran to his father, threw his arms around him, lifted the poor unsuspecting man into the air, and twirled him around like a carousel, laughing and shouting. "To Paris! To Paris!" he cried over and over again.

"He's a lunatic," the father laughed, struggling to release himself. He was so proud and pleased with his son.

"What goes on there?" his wife called from the shop.

"Be still, my son, before your mother comes in and sees these gifts." They hurriedly began shoving the presents back under the bed. The boy knelt by the side of the bed helping his father push them out of sight, and just in time before the door opened and the woman entered. Before she could question them, the boy jumped up,

took the startled woman in his arms and
twirled her around as he had done with his
father. "To Paris!" he cried. "I'm going to
Paris!"

"I tell you, he's gone mad. Now put me
down!" The good woman turned her head
and winked at her husband so that her son
could not see the gesture. "My husband, did
you not tell me that this son of ours was no
longer a child, but a man? See how he
banters and plays. He has taken leave of his
senses, and with the miller's daughter waiting
in the shop to witness his lunacy."

She was in the other room and the boy
saw her standing there in the open doorway.
He rushed out to her and swept the fragile
girl off her feet. "I'm off to Paris. I'm off to
Paris." The baker and his wife stood there
laughing. The blind man and the angel
proceeded past them into the shop and
stood near the doorway that led out onto the
street. The blind man listened, not believing
that this was the same man he had shared
the fire with.

"I will go to Paris," the lad continued, "and
see all those wonderful things." He held the
girl's hands in his. "Imagine, Rachel, I will
see the palace and the soldiers and maybe
even the king himself. I will at last see that
great and wonderful city."

The excited young girl shared his joy.
"Yes, see everything there is to see. See
everything and remember it so that you can
tell me all of it."

"I will, Rachel, I will. And I will bring you

back a present. A fine Paris present. One for my mother and father too. Even for my sister and brothers. I will bring back presents for everyone."

As the blind man listened to the happy reverie, a disturbing sound reached his ears. It was faint, indistinct, as if far off, but growing louder. He felt his way out of the shop listening intently. Inside the shop the baker called his son back to reality. "Enough of this dreaming for now. Paris will come soon enough, but there is work to be done. Load the bread into the basket and take it to the manor. Make haste, for the baron does not like his bread cold. The boy hurriedly began filling the basket with the hot loaves.

The sound was clearer now. It was the sound of carriage wheels racing over cobblestones. The blind man whose ears were more acute than others could hear the snapping of a whip urging the horses to greater speed. "Make way!" the driver shouted. "Make way!"

The boy finished loading the bread and flung the basket onto his shoulder. "Be off with you, son, and hasten your return, for the miller tells me he wishes to speak with you this night. There are good tidings in the wind this Christmas."

The blind man could hear the racing carriage almost upon him. The sound of the whip cracked in his ears, and the noise of the wheels on the cobblestones was almost deafening. "Make way! Make way!"

"I will be back before I have left," the boy

shouted.

The blind man sensed the impending danger. He turned toward the shop and shouted, "Wait! Wait!"

He was too late — not that the boy could have heard him anyway. He might have heard the carriage bearing down on him, were it not for his excitement, or his haste. He might have seen it had it not been for the huge basket of bread on his shoulder that blocked it from view. He ran into the street straight into the path of the racing horses. In an instant, they struck him down. The horses reared up, their flight suddenly stopped. Then with even greater fury they galloped on. Behind them they left the baker's son sprawled on the cobblestones.

"My God," his mother cried out, running to him. "My God, my God," over and over again. Rachel ran out behind her. "Oh no!" she cried. "No! No!" Others came running too, villagers drawn by the commotion. They gathered around the fallen boy, who lay there writhing in pain. "My leg!" he cried in unbearable agony. "My leg!"

His mother knelt in the street to gather her suffering son into her arms. As she took hold of him and drew him to her breast, his shattered leg lay facing the wrong way. His pain was unspeakably intense. Before the blessedness of unconsciousness came to him, he gave one last shout of agony. "Angel!" he cried and slipped into sleep.

He was standing there again beside the blind man and the angel, old and crippled once more. In the street, the baker picked his son up into his arms and carried him into the shop. His wife and Rachel followed after them, weeping bitterly. The crowd lingered for a while, then drifted away. As the sun set, the silent snow began to fall.

"Why have you done this to me?" the lame beggar screamed at the angel.

"It was your will," he replied.

"Was I to have found Christmas there?"

"It was your desire," he repeated. "It was there."

"Well, I did not find it," he said in anger. "I found no Christmas there."

"Christmas is not a time," the angel replied. Then he turned to the blind man. "Where is it you would look to find Christmas if that is your desire?"

The blind man pondered for a while. "Where should I find it but at Bethlehem?" he said.

"So be it," the angel announced.

IV

The three found themselves standing at the
base of a small hill not far from the entrance
to a cave. The night air was chilly. Nearby
the lights from a little village lit up the sky.

"Where are we?" asked the blind man,
sensing the change.

"In a strange place," replied the crippled
man, his eyes searching the area round
about them.

"Are we in Bethlehem?"

"There is a village not far from here if that
be Bethlehem."

What would he find here? A miracle? Did
he dare hope for it again? There is no hope
for the blind. He would not allow himself to

27

suffer such futile anguish again. His world was an arm's length. His dreams went no further than the distance he could hear. Reality had taught him that. Its weight had crushed him from his birth.

But try as he might to suppress it, the old stirring welled up within him again. His heart quickened and his flesh tingled. There was constant war being waged within him — the spirit, the fire, the temper of his father against the gentility and compassion of his mother.

Hard was bad. The walls, the trees, the fences that stopped him, hurt him, frustrated him. The clenched fist that beat him, the angry shouts that terrified him. The world and his father had taught him craftiness, cunning, and deceit.

When not doing battle against hard, there were rare moments of soft. Soft was good. Soft was animals that he loved to touch and pet. Soft was food that gave him satisfaction. Soft was warm. Soft was his mother.

"Teach him your foolish lessons, woman. Fill his empty head with your fairy tales of God and saints. He is a curse. I am cursed with an only son who cannot lighten my burden, and a wife who can bring nothing into this world but her own kind. Teach him to bear children, woman. Then maybe he can give me a son."

The woman sat there silently, the blind boy seated at her feet, his head resting in her lap. She moved quickly to cover his ears with her hands, but she was too late. The hard words

had found their mark. The boy rose and hurled himself with a frenzy toward the bowman. A quick blow on the side of the boy's head brought him down to the earthen floor. His mother hurried over to him to comfort him. He pushed her away. Hard and soft. His life was a constant struggle between hard and soft.

Later, much later, his mother told him of a strange man, a hermit, who lived not far from their village. She was going to take him there. All during the journey she told him story after story about the saints and the wonderful miracles they performed. Hope and longing burned in his heart as never before. Each moment, each step, became an agony of anticipation, until at last they stood before him.

"This is my son," she said to the holy man. "Touch him. Pray over him. Please heal him." The boy's blood raced through his body. His head throbbed, and his flesh tingled waiting for the magic touch.

It was a gentle voice that spoke hard words. "Good woman, I cannot heal. Only Jesus can heal." Soft hands held the boy's face. "My son, only Jesus can heal."

Softness began to congeal, warmth to chill. Hard. Hard. The world is hard. He must not forget this. He must never let this happen again. And yet it was happening. It was happening all over again. The words echoed in his memory. "Only Jesus can heal." This was Bethlehem and Jesus was here. His breathing quickened. His flesh tingled.

"Angel, tell me," cried the blind man, "is it Bethlehem?"

"It is."

"Then he's here. Jesus is here."

"He is here."

"I must go to him. Tell me where."

"Within," said the angel.

The crippled man had walked to the entrance of the cave and was peering in. The blind man, with his arms outstretched, stumbled towards him. "Is he there? Do you see him?"

"I see only a man and a woman," he answered.

The blind man whose hearing was ordinarily so acute was startled by strange sounds that suddenly surrounded them. It was the noise of animals totally unfamiliar to him. It was not so much a braying, as a groaning as they settled to the ground complaining loudly. Strange voices speaking a strange language filled the night air — excited voices, from the sound of it.

"What's happening? What is it?" he cried.

The crippled man had never seen camels nor the likes of the riders, so he was at a loss to describe the event. "Some travelers have stopped here," was all he could say.

The blind man searched his memory of the stories his mother had told him. These then must be the magi bringing their gifts to the infant. They walked past the two beggars as if they were not there and entered the cave. It was true, then. All that he had been told was true. His heart began to pound furiously. Touch him. Heal him. Only Jesus can heal.

The blind man stumbled into the cave. "The manger. He is in the manger," he remembered. His hands groped and at last touched the wood of the manger. It was the moment he dared not dream of, dared not hope for. With both hands trembling, he slowly, gently, reached inside.

His hands touched the hay, slowly searching for the infant. But there was no infant. His hands moved across the hay at first gently, then desperately. Nothing. They moved back and forth again quickly. Still nothing. Now they began to feel deeply into the hay; deep down to the bottom of the manger and up along the sides, searching frantically. There was no child. No softness. No warmth. Only hard.

"No!" he cried out in anguish. "No!" he cried from the very depths of his bitter soul, so that it filled the night and echoed in the valleys of his empty years. Overwhelming hard. Unbearable cold. Endless darkness.

From his misery, from his unredeemed hopelessness, from all the breath that was left in him, he cried out, "Angel!"

Once again he was standing outside the cave with the crippled man and the angel. The blind man, sensing the change, shouted at his tormentor, "Why have you done this to me?"

"It was your will," he replied.

"Was I to have found Christmas there?"

"It was your desire," he repeated. "It was there."

"Well, I did not find it," he said in anger. "I found no Christmas there."

"Christmas is not a place," the angel replied.

The crippled man quickly interrupted, "What torment is this? What madness is this? It is not here. It is not there. We are crippled and blind and you make sport of us. Is this perverted agony our judgment? Does heaven mock the infirm? If we had but eyes and sound legs. . . ."

Before he could utter another word of protest, the angel said, "So be it."

V

The air was warm, almost hot. The sun
brilliantly shining in a cloudless sky spread
its warmth and softness on the hill where the
two beggars now found themselves. They
were surrounded by people, some standing
alone, some in clusters of three and four.
There was something strange about the
place and about the gathering, the blind man
thought as he cocked his head, listening
attentively. He knew there were people about
him — many people, from the sound of
it — yet their voices were not loud or frantic
as in the marketplace or on the village
streets. They were subdued, hushed. There
was a sense of calm, of peace here.

35

"Where are we?" he asked, pivoting his head in quick movements back and forth like an animal sniffing the breeze.

"I don't know," replied the crippled man, who was himself studying the surroundings. "I do not know where we are or what place this is or what time this is."

"Ask the angel," the blind man exhorted.

"He is not here."

Still shaken from his previous ordeal and afraid of another torment at the hands of the angel, the blind man turned to his companion, pleading, "This place troubles me. We did not ask to be brought here. I fear the angel has another torment in store for us. Let us be off before it is too late."

At just that moment word was passing through the crowd for the people to sit. This made the passage of the two beggars next to impossible, for now there were people sitting and reclining everywhere.

"What is it?" cried the blind man. "Why do you hesitate?"

Ignoring his companion's pleas, but curious for his own sake, the crippled man questioned those nearest him. "What is happening?"

"The prophet is about to teach. Hush now and listen," came the impatient reply.

"Let us leave this place," pleaded the blind man. "I am afraid of the judgment that awaits us here."

"We cannot. Where would we go. We must stop and think what action we must take." So the two sat on the warm earth

36

along with the others, while the sun relaxed their bodies and a gentle breeze carried the words of the prophet over the assembled throng.

At first the beggars paid no heed, for they were lost in thoughts of their own. But the sun was shining on their bodies, and soon their minds relaxed to its warmth. The words of the speaker gently filtered into their troubled minds, easing out their futile thoughts of self-concern. It was a strong voice, yet strangely calm and peaceful, that spoke. The more the beggars listened, the more the hypnotic voice lulled them away from themselves. He spoke of love. His voice was soft but his message was strong, even peculiar. Love those who hate you. Embrace those who speak ill of you. Be kind to those who persecute you. Give to those who ask of you, even to the last measure.

While the soothing voice of the prophet warmed the chill of their memories as they reclined in the warm sun surrounded by compassionate listeners and the magic of the moment filled their hearts and minds, for just the briefest of moments, in lives filled with frustration and bitterness; the blind man thought thoughts of love for his father and the crippled man repented his countless unkindnesses to his fellow man.

While still lost in this reverie, the voice ceased speaking. Like a whisper the prophet was now making his way through the crowd. He stopped at the place where the two beggars lay. Without a word he reached his

hand to the crippled man. Now there was
no bitterness in him, no harshness or
cruelty, only a long since forgotten sense of
peace and happiness. He reached out his
hand in a rare gesture of affection and
gratitude. Without the slightest effort, the
prophet raised the beggar to his feet, almost
as if the crippled man had done so by
himself. Again without a word, he reached
down and placed his hand over the eyes of
the blind man. Then he turned and
proceeded through the crowds down the hill.

The crippled man stood there awestruck
for some moments. Suddenly the realization
came to him that he was standing without
the support of his crutch. Disbelieving, he
gently shifted his weight to his crippled leg. It
stood. It stood firm. My God, it didn't buckle.
He lifted his good leg so as to test the bad
one, just to make sure. It withstood the test.
He looked down at the leg. It was no longer
twisted, no longer maimed. It was sound and
whole again. His joy was uncontrollable. With
a shout of exultation, he jumped up into the
air. "I'm healed! I'm healed!" he repeated
over and over again. "I can walk! I'm
healed!" He was a boy again, shouting and
jumping outside his father's bakery shop.

The blind man sat there listening, yet not
totally. His eyes felt strangely different. It was
a feeling he had never experienced before.
They began to itch or tingle, so he started
rubbing them. Something was happening.
An unfamiliar whiteness began to penetrate
the blackness that was his life's companion.

How could he speak of it? How could he describe it? It was something he had never known. His companion's shouts of joy were but distant echoes of his own growing excitement. Blurs. Blurs that made him want to scream, to cry, to shout out. He blinked and blinked again. The images became clearer. At last it happened. He could see. He could see clearly now. He could see the crippled man jumping up and down for joy. He could see the crowds of people gathering around them, watching the miracle that was taking place. He could see the trees and the deep blue sky with its blazing sun above him. He slowly raised his hands before his face and with a cry that could be heard into eternity, he screamed from the depths of his soul: "I can see!"

The two men were completely circled now by a growing crowd of excited people. The beggars' excitement was contagious. The peace and quiet of moments before was replaced with the growing sounds of joy and merriment. As the crippled man jumped and leapt with amazement, so too did the onlookers in happy imitation. The blind man with his new-found sight asked endless questions. "What is this?" "What is that?" The fact that they answered him in a language totally unfamiliar to him and he understood was a miracle lost in the excitement of seeing for the very first time in his life. The merriment continued for hours.

At long last the crowd dispersed and the two beggars, delightfully exhausted, were left

40

alone with each other.

"What now?" asked the crippled man as they watched the crowds slowly drift away.

"Tell me," said the blind one. "Who was it that healed us?"

"They say he was a prophet, a holy one of God."

"So he must have been to have done this wondrous thing to us. Even as he spoke, I was filled with a peace I have never known in my life. That alone would have been miracle enough. But tell me, now that I can see, what did he look like?"

"I don't know," said the crippled man. "I cannot say. For when he spoke he stood at the top of the hill there and was too far away to make out clearly."

"But when he came to us, surely you must have seen him."

"I gave no thought to it, for I myself felt strangely different after listening to his words. When he stood there to take my hand I could not see his face, for the sun shone brilliantly behind him and I was blinded by its light. Afterward, in truth, I was so excited that I gave no further thought to him. I tell you, if I were to see him this moment, I would not recognize him."

"We are both of us indebted to him as to no one else on the face of this earth, and alas, we do not know who he is, save a prophet."

"It is regrettable," said the crippled man. "But so be it. We are restored." Then as if the weight of their present situation suddenly pressed itself upon him, now that the strangeness and the excitement were over, he asked again, "What now?"

The blind man had been too excited to ponder such a practical question. The force of it suddenly struck him too. What were they to do? Indeed where were they? What was to happen to them now? Such thoughts naturally brought to mind the angel who had brought them to this miraculous event. "The angel," he thought. "Where is the angel?"

"We must summon the angel," he replied.

"I don't know where he is, for he was not with us when we arrived here."

"Let us summon him as we did before."

"Angel!" they cried into the fading sunlight, and, then again, "Angel!" as the evening shadows lengthened and the night chill settled about them.

A solitary figure suddenly appeared descending the hill. At length he stood before them. "What is it you wish?" he asked.

"We want to go home," said the crippled man now cured.

"It will be as you wish," said the angel. "But I must tell you. When you return all things will be as they were then."

"You mean I will be crippled again?" shouted the cripple after pondering the import of his words.

"All things will be as they were then," repeated the angel.

"If I return, I will be blind again?"

"You will be blind," the angel replied.

There was a long silence. Each weighed what the angel's message would mean. The lame man thought of what it would be like to once again be crippled. To grovel at the feet of haughty noblemen. To beg again from disdainful merchants. To connive, to cheat, to steal. To drag a useless leg through a life of misery. Why return?

The blind man thought of his new-found vision. What was there to return to? To darkness? To cold? To bitterness? Life there was hard; endless hard. Why return?

The crippled man spoke first. His past had caught up with him. His memory of all that was happening mingled with the shrewdness of a methodically honed, crafty mind. "Once again you have tricked us, angel," he charged.

"I have not tricked you. I have done as you have wished. You asked for your youth and it was granted. You asked for Bethlehem and it too was granted. Yet you persisted and complained of your lameness and blindness, and now that too has been taken care of as you wished."

"Yet you torment us by telling us that we may not return home without the loss of these things we have grieved for." His mind was racing now. Gone was the naiveté of new-found joy. It was being replaced by the cunning shrewdness of a well-tutored past. He remembered that the angel had come for judgment. So this was to be his judgment — an endless purgatory of futile hope and despairing frustration. He would not allow himself to be bested. He would outwit his tormentor — yes, even his judgment. He was clever enough, and he would use the angel's own words to trap him.

"I will remain here," he announced. "What need do I have to return to a beggar's role while here I am sound and once again fleet of foot? I will remain here." As he spoke, he kept thinking to himself that if he were to return, judgment would surely come to him at that moment as the angel had proclaimed. To remain here would be to stall his judgment, and he resolved to forestall it for as long as possible.

"So be it," said the angel. Then, turning to the blind man, he asked, "And you?"

What was he to do. Could he return to a life of sightless beggary now that he experienced the joys that vision offered him. The hope that he had dared not even think about since he was a boy was now fulfilled. What was there to return to. Yet, somehow, he felt strangely ill at ease when he said to the angel, "I will remain."

"It will be as you both wish," said the angel. "So be it." Then he disappeared.

VI

The world is not cold and difficult only to
those who are blind. Its hardness goes
beyond the reach of an arm's length.
Dreams are shattered far beyond the
distance of one's hearing. Nor is Christmas
found in the strength of legs made whole
again.

The two beggars, now healed of their
physical wounds, made their way into the
city. They remained together, no longer
because of their infirmities, but because they
were foreigners in a strange land. They had
chosen to remain, and never to return to
familiar places with their all too familiar
hardships. This price was meager enough to

47

pay for a new life with new limbs and new
hope. A strange city and foreign ways can be
mastered and made familiar when one has
eyes to see and strong legs to walk.

As they entered the city, they were
recognized by those who had been on the
hill. People everywhere came flocking to
them to hear the wondrous account of their
miraculous healing. Each day they would sit
for hours recounting their tale to the different
groups of people who had gathered for the
telling. In gratitude these would share their
homes and their tables with the beggars, for
they were a people given to tales of prophets
and heroes and not altogether unkind to
strangers. The beggars too were careful to
say nothing about the angel and their
strange odyssey lest the people consider
them lunatics or charlatans and they lose the
hospitality to which they had grown
accustomed.

But tales grow tired in the telling and
listeners become increasingly disinterested
with each repetition. In time there was no one
left to listen and no more hospitality to be
given. The beggars once again found
themselves alone and abandoned.

"What now?" said the man who had been
cured of his blindness.

"Since we are fated to remain here, we
must make for ourselves a new life," replied
his companion.

This was far easier said than done in that
strange land. For here they were foreigners
and no one would give them work. Even the

crippled man's experience as a baker was
useless to him, for in this land the bread was
strange and different. The blind man could
offer no better, for indeed he had never
worked gainfully in his entire life.

Once again idleness piqued at their spirits
and hunger at their bellies. As the spirit
yielded, the body became more demanding.
Perhaps the onslaught was too great or their
new spirit too unformed to withstand the test.
Perhaps they had no other experiences or
resources to fall back upon than the clever
wiles of beggars' ways. Whatever the reason,
in order to feed the body and sustain the
spirit, they were forced once again to resort
to begging.

Alas even in this difficult humiliating
decision there was to be no respite.
Passers-by would not give alms to beggars
with sound bodies. Instead they jeered and
ridiculed them as sluggards and parasites.
The people had a perverse penchant for
derogatory descriptions. They were heckled
as "foreign vermin" and the "Romans'
dung."

Their last state had become far worse than
their first. In their homeland, they were at
least accepted; here they were rejected. In
their homeland they were familiar with the
people's ways and conscience; here prophets
and religious teachers abounded, yet the
mendicant was disdained as an outcast of
God. In their homeland they were blind and
crippled yet could survive; here their bodies
were whole but they were perishing. At home

they could beg; here they resolved that they must steal.

Old habits would now become the pattern for new crime. They knew well the ways of the blind and the crippled. This time-learned experience, now feigned, would easily pass the test of the most critical observer. So it was that the blind man with eyes closed tight was blind again and the crippled man with crutch and dragging leg was lame once more. The deception was perfect.

They worked as a team, as partners in crime. They would enter the marketplace amid the crush and confusion of busy shoppers as two stricken beggars beseeching alms. The blind man would approach an unsuspecting merchant, in short order relieve him of his purse (an art in which the crippled man had carefully tutored him, having been no stranger to such practices in his lifetime) and relay it to the crippled man waiting nearby. He in turn would limp away behind the stalls, quickly run a short distance and re-emerge in the marketplace once again to await the approach of his companion. Who would suspect a blind man? How would a blind man know where a man's purse was? Even if they observed him, his blind act was flawless. Even when they searched him, which happened only infrequently, they found nothing. At times they would work the routine in reverse lest the blind man's presence at so many thefts draw suspicion. They were careful never to be seen in public

together so as never to draw attention to their alliance.

With the passing days they grew increasingly more adept in their art. As beggar-thieves they prospered. At last, however, the day of reckoning came. The blind man had snatched the purse of a high official. The procurator never walked among the people without his bodyguard a short distance off observing his every move. As they closed in to apprehend the thief, they were delayed just long enough to see him pass the purse to his crippled confederate. So it was that they were both seized and arrested.

Judgment was swift and harsh. It was the procurator himself who sentenced them to death. The soldiers marched the beggars out of the city to the hill of execution. Many of the victims of their crimes followed in procession, jeering and taunting them, eagerly awaiting the solace of final retribution. At the summit of the hill, the thieves were crucified.

As they hung on their crosses in agony, the crowd heaped further scorn upon them, yelling vulgarities, cursing, mocking their infirmities, and spitting at them. The crippled man who had little regard for people had even less for these his tormentors. With practiced adroitness he shouted back invective for invective, curse for curse. The scene was a tableau of hell. The blind man awaited his end in silence. He thought the clamor would never end. He wished to die in peace.

As if they had heard his wish and were responding to his last desire, the people suddenly became quiet, for a commotion further down the hill had distracted them. A crowd was approaching. As it drew nearer, the clamor became louder, more distinct. It was a haunting replay of their own experience. Another man was being led to execution.

When they reached the summit the prisoner was stripped and nailed to his cross. Once again the blind man's ears were filled with the cruel sounds of the venomous crowd. Once again there were the taunts and the jeers.

"Prophet, come down from the cross," they shouted.

"Come down. Then we'll believe you," they laughed.

The blind man watched and listened, but the prisoner gave no response. From the shouts of the crowd he could fathom no cause for this man's execution. What had he done? Why were they mocking him?

Barely audible above the din of the crowd, the first words of the prisoner reached him: "Father, forgive them; they do not know what they are doing."

The crowd responded in a frenzy of mockery: "The king forgives us. He is a king; see his crown." Then came derisive laughter. "He saved others," they said. "Let him save himself if he is the Chosen One of God."

With each new taunt, the crowd became silent so as not to miss a word, as if to savor each encounter. The blind man was startled to hear his crippled companion speak. For a moment he had forgotten their own plight. The words he heard somehow echoed in his memory.

"Are you not a prophet?" the crippled beggar shouted mockingly to the delight of the crowd. "Save yourself and us as well."

For a fleeting moment, in the instant before he spoke up himself, the blind man thought, "Strange that he would think of me. The crippled man never thought of anyone but himself." But the distraction passed quickly as he turned to his companion and said, "Have you no fear of God at all? We have received the same sentence as this man, but we deserve it. We are paying for what we did. This man has done nothing wrong."

"Fear God!" the crippled man shouted back. "If that man is of God, then I say: Let him come down from that cross and save me. I am sick of this place, this wretched country and these perverse people. They call themselves God's chosen ones and they hail more prophets than there are stones in the desert. They are simpletons and fools no less than the one who hangs here before us."

The crowd watched in silence as if relishing this dissension among thieves. The blind man would listen to no more of this. He turned to the prisoner. "Prophet. Remember me when you enter into your kingdom."

The prisoner leaned his head back,

straining to speak directly to the blind man. "Indeed, I promise you," he replied, "today you will be with me in paradise."

Despite the murmurings of the crowd, the prophet's voice could be heard clearly. The crowd heard it. So too did the crippled man. It was the first time he had unmistakably heard his voice. Somehow it was familiar. He had heard that voice before. It was a haunting voice that reached deep into his memory. His mind raced through the voices of many memories, as waves breaking on the shore in a violent storm. As he neared his destination his heart quickened and his flesh tingled in anticipation. Yes, there it was once again — on the hill where the angel had left them. It was the voice of the prophet — the prophet who had reached out to him, the prophet who had gently lifted him, healed him. It was the same one. It was Jesus.

"No!" he screamed in torment at the realization of what he had done. "No!" he cried out in agony and despair as the wind blew and heavy pellets of rain beat heavenly punishment on him and the dispersing crowd. His voice was barely heard amid the growing peals of thunder and the deep rumblings of the earth quaking beneath him, when from the depths of all his remaining anguish, he screamed: "Angel!"

VII

The night air was bone-chilling cold now that
the fire had breathed the last of its
impoverished warmth. The crippled man lay
writhing on the ground while the blind man,
once again sightless, stood transfixed as if
frozen by the night air. In the distance, the
village clock of Soissons pealed the hour of
midnight. The familiar sound stirred the blind
beggar out of his trance. "What is that?
Where are we?" He stumbled in the
darkness, reaching out, searching once
again. "Are we home?"

The voice of his companion startled the
prostrate beggar. He sat up quickly like one
jolted to reality from the throes of a violent

57

nightmare. It was a dream, he thought. It was all a dream.

"Am I alone? Is anyone here?" the voice pleaded.

The crippled man could not yet speak. His heart was still beating furiously, and the blood was pounding in his temples. It was but a dream, and here I sit frightened like a child, he thought. The realization calmed him. His bravado returned.

"You are not alone, blind one. I am here."

"What happened?" the blind man turned toward the direction of his comforter.

"I fell asleep, that's all."

"But what of the angel? Where is the angel?"

What manner of madness is this, the crippled man thought. How could this beggar know of my dreams? I must have called out in my sleep. In truth he had done so a great many times in his youth when dreams of his misfortune haunted his sleep. But he had not done so in years. He had become too guarded, too strong-minded to allow such weakness to recur. He must not let this blind beggar know this weakness. "What angel? What are you talking about?"

"The angel of Christmas. The angel of judgment."

How much did he shout out in his sleep? How much had this beggar heard? "There is no angel," he growled. "Stop your foolish talk."

But the blind man would not be silenced. "The angel who brought us to your youth

58

when the carriage crushed your leg. The angel who took us to Bethlehem."

Could it be? Could this have happened? Once again his heart began to quicken. Would this blind man never be still?

"Have you forgotten?" his tormentor pleaded. "Have you forgotten the Holy One who healed us? Have you forgotten" — he paused, the memory painful — "the crucifixion?"

The crippled man sat on the ground dumbstruck. My God, it was no dream. It had happened. It had truly happened to the two of them. "What madness has come to us this night?" he shouted.

"No, my friend. Not madness. Mercy. Judgment. Merciful judgment has come to us this blessed night. It was as the angel had said."

"But we did not find Christmas." His tone had changed. His bravado was gone. He was a child again.

"Remember what the angel said: "This night it has been given to you to find Christmas if you so wish it."

"We did so wish," pleaded the crippled man, "but instead we found anguish."

The blind man paused, straining to recall the angel's words. The solution to the mystery was somewhere locked in his statements. "Christmas is not a time or a place," he repeated.

"Nor did we find it in the healing of our bodies," the crippled man pondered, further unraveling the mystery.

The full realization suddenly came to the blind man. It was clear to him now — the angel, the message, all that had happened to them. It made sense; it was unmistakably clear.

"It was the touch," he shouted out with joy. "It was his touch."

The crippled man had not arrived yet. "But he touched us and we are still here waiting," he pleaded.

"Yes, he touched us. But now we must touch him." The blind man stood, his arms outstretched to heaven, lost in his discovery. "But how? We are no longer there and he is not here."

In the distance the clock tower had finished striking the hour of twelve. There was a holy stillness in the night air. Gradually, from far off, the sweet, peaceful sound of chant began to fill the air. In the abbey midnight Mass had begun.

The blind man turned toward salvation. His face shone with the beatific vision. "He is here," he rejoiced. "This night, the angel said, this night."

"Where? Where is he?"

"In the church," he said pointing to the music. "He is in the church. Quick! Let us go to him! Let us touch him! Christmas awaits us."

The crippled man struggled to his feet. He bent over for his crutch. When he lifted it he saw that it had been severed in two. His heart leapt for joy. It was true. It was all true.

"Wait," he called out to his companion. "I

have no crutch." The blind man turned to him. "I will be your crutch," he announced. "And I will be your eyes," the crippled man replied. The two beggars took hold of one another and arm in arm they hastened toward the abbey.

VIII

Within the abbey church the bishop was
seated on his throne while the choir finished
the last Kyrie. A hush fell over the assembled
worshipers. In the right transept the tableau
of the nativity mirrored the holy scene of
Bethlehem. All was now as it was then
except for the Christ Child. There was no
infant. The manger stood empty. God would
provide, the bishop had said, but as of yet he
had not. There would be no Gloria without
the infant, no bells without Jesus. Everyone
waited in silence.

The huge doors of the abbey church
creaked open. The two beggars entered. "We
are here," announced the crippled man

63

leaning heavily on his blind companion. The blind man struggling under his weight gasped. "Where is he? Where is he?" he repeated over and over again. They proceeded slowly down the center aisle, the lame man searching desperately, longingly. As they reached the front of the cathedral he saw the living crèche. "He is here!" he shouted. "It is Bethlehem!" The blind man reached out his arms, searching. His companion fell to the stone floor.

"Where?" he pleaded, walking aimlessly.

"In front of you! In front of you!" he shouted, dragging his twisted leg across the floor toward the manger.

The blind man stumbled forward until his hands touched the wood of the manger. Once again, he was at Bethlehem. This time he knew Jesus would be there.

The crippled man, exhausted from his effort and spent from his long night's experience, lay breathlessly at the foot of the manger. This time he knew Jesus would be here.

The blind man reached slowly, gently into the crib. The crippled man, propped on his elbow, reached up his arm and gently reached into the manger.

"He is here!" cried the blind man. "Jesus is here!" Tears of joy streamed down his face.

To the crippled man the touch of Jesus was unmistakable. "It is Jesus!" he shouted. Once again that peace flooded into his soul. It would never again leave now that he had

found him. He wept no longer for himself but for joy. "It is Jesus!" he sobbed.

At this announcement of his presence, the bells in the abbey steeple began to ring out for joy. The bishop stood in full pontifical splendor and intoned, "Gloria in excelsis Deo." The choir burst forth its response as if all the heavenly hosts had joined them in the celebration. The cathedral walls echoed joyously the ringing bells, the angelic polyphony, the good news: "Jesus is here!"

There at the manger, transfixed in glory, were the two heralds of this great event. And there inside the manger was nothing else but the hand of the blind beggar and the hand of the crippled beggar clasped tightly together.